Logan's Logic: Life Thr Eyes of a Retired Gre

By

Logan Auty Houghton

Fank yous to . . .

Wendy Lewis for Kicking Daddy up the bum and making him write the book.

Lynn Auty (Mummy) and Karl Houghton (Daddy) for making me the most loved houndie in the world.

Nanna Margaret for all the treat's goodies and cuddles.

e.j.oakes.

Finally, Fank yous to all the people around the world who have followed my journey and have helped make this book possible.

Loves --

Logan The Houndie.

PROLOGUE

Saturday afternoon and I was with Mum shopping at the local retail park when we came across a local greyhound charity doing some fundraising. As we have had greyhounds from as far back as the late 1970's we can't help but take a look. We started chatting about the hounds with the volunteers and then we saw him, A beautiful black dog! Mum says, "He's stunning and would suit you and Lynn down to the ground!"

"His name is Logan" a volunteer says. I whirled round to come face to face with my old friend and sometime comedian Kenny Mills.

"Oh, Hiya Karl, I didn't know it was you, how's things?"

We had a chat about old times and the conversation turned to the rescue.

"You know a lot about greyhounds Karl, how do you fancy volunteering with the dog walking and fundraising?"

"Yeah, I'm up for it," I reply. I asked about the black dog and Kenny replies, "Oh you mean Logan? He's a lovely dog and a favourite with all the volunteer walkers, mainly because he's bonkers!"

Ma was still smitten with him, thinks we should have taken him home there and then, but I took the details and offered my services as a walker. The following week I finished work early enough to walk with the rescue. I turned up and who should be there but Kenny: "Oh, hiya Karl, I've got just the dog for you to walk, ta da! Here he is, it's Logan!"

Knowing that Kenny could sell snow to the Eskimos I should have seen it coming, shouldn't I? Doh! After a couple of walks I convinced Lynn to come down with me and she gets involved too. I found out that Logan had been in the kennels longer than all the other dogs because he was a bit 'bonkers'. Everyone seemed to love him for it, but no one wanted to take the chance and give him a home.

After about 3 weeks of walking Logan, I took a leap of faith and decided to take him home for the weekend to give him some time in a house. We were given a lead, a muzzle, a raincoat, some food for him and his favourite toy, which happened to be a doggy tyre that he would show everyone who came to the kennels in the hope they would pick him to take home.

He gets into the house and promptly pees on the side of the couch! I think to myself, "Aaargh! What have I done?"

Lynn shakes her head and says, "It's a good job it's leather eh?!", and goes to get a cloth and some warm soapy water to clean it down. Not an inauspicious start eh dog!

I have to say that he never once peed in the house after that. As it was a Friday night, we would normally have gone to the pub but with our 'new arrival' we didn't bother. We were happy to walk him and spend the night in front of the TV. Bedtime arrived and we left him on his duvet with his tyre and some other toys we just "happened to buy for him." Ten minutes after going to bed the whining starts.

"Maybe he needs a pee and a poop?" Lynn says.

"He'll be fine because he's only just been out and besides, he has the run of the house." I replied. Lynn took no notice and went down to take him for a walk. To cut a long story short, for the first night this scenario was repeated about 10 times! Me, I slept through it all because I knew he was in new surroundings, in a strange place and if we left him he would of eventually settled down. The following night he did exactly that and of course, mum came up about 3 times just to make sure everything was alright with the new 'baby.'

Sunday evening came round and it was time for his short holiday in a home to end - or so we thought - Lynn packed up all his doggy stuff in preparation for his return in the morning. 3am on the Monday morning, my alarm went off so I threw myself out of bed and went to work. All the time I was thinking about Logan and will he be okay going back to the kennels? About 10am and the truck phone rang, it was Lynn in tears! "I can't face him going back and staying in the rescue so I'm going down now to adopt him and I will bring him back home with me."

NOW THE FUN BEGINS!

We had Logan for about 10 days and although we live right in the centre of town, we were only about 200 yards from open fields, some lovely walks and the local golf club. As it was early summer it was a breath of fresh air for both of us being out with an inquisitive dog. One nice sunny evening Lynn decided she would take him out alone to see how he reacted with her on her own. Forty-five minutes later she walks in, takes the lead off Logan and stomps upstairs. Logan meanwhile wanders into the kitchen to get a drink and something to eat. Halfway upstairs she stops, turns to me and tells me she has never been so embarrassed in her life, then continues upstairs to take off her shoes then returns to tell her tale of woe.

"I walked down to the golf club and across the car park a gentleman is leaning against his car removing his golf shoes after playing a round. We say "good evening" to each other and I carried on walking.

"Excuse me Miss," he says, I turned around and asked, "Yes can I help you?"

"Errrm, could I possibly have my shoe back?"

I notice he isn't looking at me but he's staring at Logan and I look down to see him with the guys £200 golf shoe in his mouth!!

"I'm ever so sorry we've only had him about a week and we're just learning each other's quirks."

Some weeks later and Logan is able to go 'off lead' in certain places. We head for a late-night walk through the park in the centre of town where he could run around and burn off some energy. On the way back we went through what we dubbed 'Pussycat Alley', got to the other end where he could go 'off lead' again. It was late at night so it was dark and Logan was about 10 yards in front of us when he looked down a side road and his ears suddenly pricked up! I caught him up to see what he was looking at and there it was, a black cat! He was off in hot pursuit, as fast as his paws would carry him, the cat turned a corner and disappeared into a driveway with Logan about 10 yards behind (It's a tarmac road so his turning circle isn't that great). He managed to turn himself 90 degrees and he disappeared too, there was an almighty crashing and banging then silence! Lynn was halfway down the road by this time while I stood there waiting for the outcome. What seemed like a lifetime later Logan came trotting back proud as punch with something in his mouth. Lynn was mortified but Logan was having none of it, gave her a wide berth with his 'Prize'. Lynn was shouting, "I think he's got that cat! Oh my god what are we going to do?"

I peered into the darkness as he heads my way. "It was the wrong colour, it was a black cat and this is white."

Lynn replied, "What is it then?"

I shout to Logan and he sheepishly walked towards me then stopped: "Come here fella let's have a look at what you've got." I managed to grab his collar but he was not for giving up his prize. I started to wrestle it off him while Lynn made her way back toward me. I guess, I could have told Lynn sooner but it was just too funny!

"What has he got Karl? It had better not be that bloody cat!"

"Nope, it is a roast chicken!" He had probably stolen it off the table in that house. We both looked at each other and decided it was time for a sharp exit!

Life with Logan began in such a crazy way and so it continued.

Read on and enjoy the book --

Karl . . .

Follow me on -- https://www.facebook.com/logan.autyhoughton

One . . .

"Daddy!"

"Ugh, err. Yes Logan?"

"Is you asleeps?"

"I'm not now am I?"

"I wuz just checking."

"What's up Logan?"

"Is you hoomans cleverer than us hounds?"

"Hmm. That depends I suppose."

"Well, I was watching that telly fingy in the corner and some hoomans came on a fing called "The Jeremy Kyle show.""

"Aah well you see Logan it's like this . . .."

"Nevermind daddy. Oh, while you're awake."

"Well I wasn't but I am now aren't I Logan."

"Yes you are daddy. Now, as I was saying, while you're awake could you lets me out coz I needs a pee and a poop?"

"Yes of course I can. Is there anything else I can do for you?"

"Yes. Can you give my dinner a stir and I'll have a couple of treats when I gets back?"

"Fine. Will that be all?"

"Yep. Oh and fank yous for answering my question."

"Wait a minute. What question?"

"The one about you hoomans being cleverer than us hounds."

"I didn't."

"I woke you ups, you is going to lets me out, then you are gonna stir my dinner and gives me treats. I finks you answered my question."

"Aaaargh! Outsmarted again!"

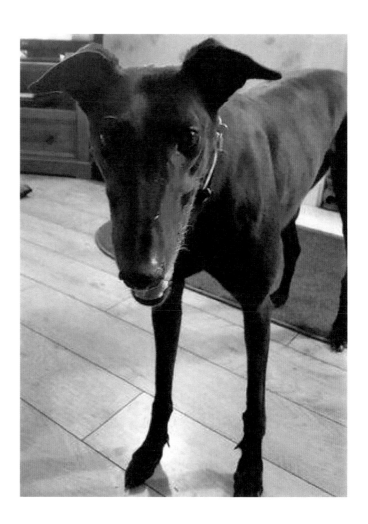

Two . . .

"Here Logan I have something for you."

"Whats is it daddy?"

"It's a treat."

"Cans I eats it?"

"Yes of course you can."

"What is it?"

"It's a local delicacy."

"Is you sure I cans eat it?"

"Yep it's fine."

"It doesn't look it!"

"Logan, you have eaten day old pizza that you found in the park before now so I wouldn't worry."

"What is it?"

"It's Bury black pudding. They are the finest in the country."

"Ok I'll gives it a go."

"Logan! What on earth are you doing?"

"Well, first of all you told me it's a treat. Then you told me it's a delicacy but I doesn't know what that is. Then you tolds me to Bury the black pudding so that's what I is doing. Silly hooman."

"No, Logan. It's a Bury black pudding."

"Exactly! So now that's what I is doing. I will saves it for laters."

"No dear dog, it's a black pudding that was made in the town of Bury just up the road from here.

"That isn't what you said tho is it."

"Logan son, some days you drive me to despair."

"I knows and sometimes you drives me to the woods so we can go for long walks."

"Don't start dog coz I'm not even going there."

"What, no more driving to the woods and no more walks???"

"Just eat the damned black pudding Logan!"

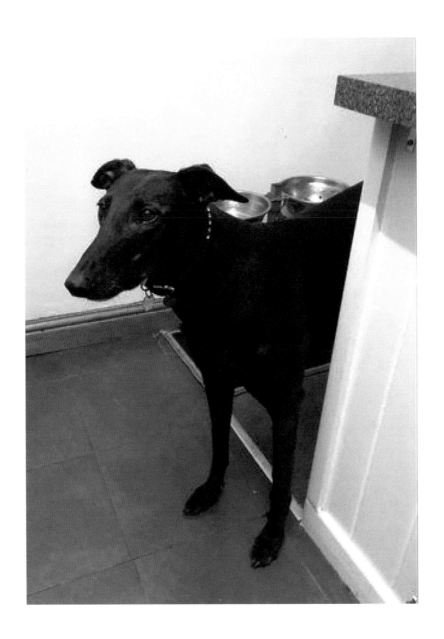

Three . . .

"Daddy can I ask you a question?"

"Yes of course you can Logan."

(I know I'm gonna regret this.)

"Does my bum look big?"

"What?"

"Well, I know I is getting a little older and sometimes things droop a little bit."

"It's fine Logan. You get plenty of exercise and you're in tip top shape."

"Is it as big as mummys?"

"Errrm." (I'm about to get shot by both sides here!) It's fine. Trust me."

"So I can carries on having treats?"

"Yes, as long as you get plenty of exercise."

"If mummy shares her pizza with me we won't gets fat?"

"Nope, it's fine." (phew! I think I dodged a bullet there.)

"But, but can I?"

"No more talking Logan. Just run along to nanna's."

"Yaay more treats! Am I as old as nanna?"

"Logan please don't dig anymore holes for me!"

"I is just asking."

"Don't you have peemails to read?"

"Aah yes. Fanks daddy."

Aah, the trials and tribulations of living with a smart assed dog!

Four . . .

"Aah, Good morning Logan."

"Can I goes out coz I needs a pee and poop?"

"Just hang on a minute dog."

"What's up now hooman?"

"Have you any idea what time it is?"

"Don't be silly hooman. I is a dog so I cants wear a watch because it slips off my paw."

"Well let me tell you. It's 10 am in the morning!"

"Aand that means what? Again. I is a dog and has no concept of time."

"You know what time it is when you need feeding!"

"Yes because my tummy tells me. Now, is I going outs?"

"Listen dog. You have been in bed since 11 pm last night. That's 11 hours!!"

"So now I needs a pee and poop. C'mon lets go because I is cross pawed here!"

"I've been up since 7 am why didn't you come down earlier?"

"Because I didn't needs a pee and poop then dids I stoopid hooman."

Five . . .

"Aah, good evening Logan."

"OK, where am I?"

"You're on your bed."

"Why is I sat up?"

"Youve been dreaming."

"What about?"

"I have no idea. You were barking and running in your sleep."

"Oh right. Dids I catch it?"

"I think you must have done."

"Why is I sat up?"

"I've already told you."

"I has no idea where I am."

"You're on your . . . Oh go back to sleep."

" I has been asleep?"

"Aaargh. Why can't we have a normal dog like everyone else!!"

Six . . .

"So Logan. I see you're back from nanna's then."

"Yep."

"I don't suppose you unpacked your case by any chance?"

"Now don't be silly hooman. For one, I doesn't do menial tasks, that's your job. And for two, I has paws not hands!"

"Aah yes I was forgetting. Silly me. So did we have a nice time down there?"

"It was my day off! I goes to nanna's to be spoiled and waited on hand and paw. Alls I did was lounge around on the bed and get fed."

"Well now we're on the subject of food . . . Did you have any treats? Remember you're on a diet! Don't be telling me porky pies or your nose will grow just like Pinocchio's did."

"Dids you just mention pork pies!!"

"It's just rhyming slang for Lies. Don't be getting excited."

"Oh. If you puts it that way, I only had one or two treats."

"Are you sure?"

"Yep. I only hads my breakfast and dinner."

"Well, what about those hot dog sausages Nanna put in your dinner?

"You can't count those! They wuz part of my dinner!!"

"They still count Logan."

"Nope they doesn't! Besides who told you?"

"Nanna said that you wouldn't eat your dinner so she had to put hot dogs in before you would eat them. Ha. Busted!!

"Grrrrr: Grassed up by Nanna! You can't trust anyone nowadays!"

Seven . . .

"Hooman you're late!"

"What?"

"You're late!"

"Late Logan? Late for what?"

"No, You're late wivs my sammiches!"

"I'm sorry but I had to work later today and the traffic was bad."

"Look hooman, my sammiches arrives no later than 4.30 in the afternoon and it's now 5pm. I'm not a happy bunny!"

"Nope you're an unhappy greyhound. "

"Laugh all you want to coz I is gonna eat these tuna mayonnaise sammiches and wipes my muzzle all over the furniture." "

"You're too smart for your own good Logan"

"I knows, but you loves me."

"Grrrrr smartass dog!"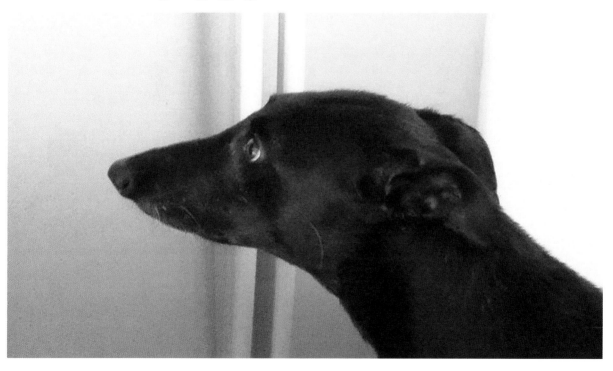

Eight . . .

"Mummy"

"What's up Logan?"

"Why is daddy in Jail?"

"He isn't. He's in FB jail. It's different."

"Why is he there then?"

"Because he's a numpty!"

"Is I a numpty?"

"No Logan. You're a smartass. There's a difference."

"Can I has a treat?"

"Nope. You've had enough today. Besides, You're on a diet for a few days because you'ra a tad overweight."

"But I fought you said I had a smartass?"

"No, I said YOU ARE a smartass not, you have a smartass. Again, there is a difference."

"So can I has a treat then?"

"NO! You are fast becoming a pain in the ass now go. Go on, out of the dining room with you."

"So, I is a smartass and a pain in the ass?"

"Yes Logan, and if you don't move, I'm going to paddle your ass!

Nine . . .

"Ok hooman. How long is this going to continue?"

"What's up now Logan?"

"How long will I be going wivsout treats?"

"Until you look less like a black Labrador and more like a black greyhound!" 😄

"Not funny hooman! Now where is my treats?"

"Look dog, You're not starving are you. Besides, you do get treats, just not as many as you used to."

" No I doesn't. I is getting very thin. In fact I is almost wasting away!"

"Ha. I don't think so. Anyway, what about the sammiches you get every day?"

"They is just a snack that you gives me when you gets in. If I remembers rightly you only gave them to me to hides the fact that you hadn't eaten your work sammiches from mummy. I was doing you a favour by eating them."

"Oh you're good dog. Come to think of it, that sounds like blackmail!"

"I is a black male greyhound."

"No Logan. That's not . . . Oh nevermind."

"Nevermind what?"

"Wait a minute! Didn't you snaffle two choccy biccies of mine last night? If I recall I'd brought them to bed and put them on the bedside cabinet and while I filled YOUR weeble up with treats YOU took 2 of the 3 biccies!"

"Well there you have it hooman. I is that starvinks I has to resort to snaffling treats because you won't gives them to me!!

Ten . . .

"Daddy."

"Yes Logan."

"Is I losing weight?"

"Well son, we can finally see a couple of ribs."

"WHAT!!"

"Yep. You're losing weight."

"Ifs you can see my ribs I must be starvinks!"

"Oh I doubt that dog."

"I has had nearly no treats for ages."

"Yes you have. You still get your sammiches when I come home."

"They isn't treats, they is food!"

"Do you remember the hillside dog show on Saturday?"

"Yes. I didn't gets any treats there. I worked all day for nuffink!"

"I remember an old gentleman stroking you. What did he say?"

"That I wuz a beautiful black doggy?"

"What he actually said was . . . What a beautiful black dog. Is he a LABRADOR??" 🤣🤣

"Short sighted old duffer! Humph."

Eleven . . .

"Morning Logan."

"Morning daddy."

"What are you doing in the back of the car Logan?"

"It's Sunday morning."

"And?"

"We always goes for walks on Sunday wivs my houndie friends."

"I thought you hounds had no concept of time?"

"That's what you hoomans thinks."

"So why the back of the car?"

"Well. Normally around this time on a Sunday Conrad comes wivs treats but he hasn't arrived so I'm guessing he's away at the caravan for a few days?"

"Riiight."

"Spit it out hooman."

"Yes he is Logan."

"Now, doesn't Denise call wivs Lexi the French bulldog before we goes?"

"Yes she does."

"She hasn't called either so she must be wivs her miniature hoomans. Am I right?"

"You mean her grandchildren. Yes she is."

"You and mummy is at homes so we is going walking. That's why I is in the back of the car."

"What about . . .

"No 'ifs or buts' daddy. It must be Sunday so we is going walking! Now call my doggy friends, go gets my lead and some poop bags and let's be off!"

"Would sir be needing a Jacket?"

"Nope I shalls be fine fank yous."

"My pleasure Lord Logan."

Twelve . . .

"Daddy what is you doing?"

"I'm having YOUR ride detailed and valeted."

"It's about time!"

"Eh?"

"Well. The back of the car was full of muddy prints and the windows wuz full of dirty marks!"

"Yes and they all belong to you!"

"Anyways. I shall lie here in the shade and supervise the whole operation."

"Yes you do that Logan."

"DADDY!"

"Yes Logan."

"I has been snow foamed!"

"That's because you got in the way dog."

"I was inspecting the job!"

"No. You poked your nose in."

"I has to make sure fings are done right."

"You're a sight hound ain't you?"

"Yes I is daddy."

"Well do it from over there."

"Daddy."

"What is it now Logan?"

"I is warm."

"Well I'll cool you down with a shower then you can go and lie in the shade."

"Will the shower includes water? You knows I doesn't like that stuff."

"How else can I shower you?"

"You can shower me wivs love. You can shower me wivs treats."

"Water will have to do dog."

"I isn't happy abouts that."

"I should have left you at home."

"Then who would have made sure MY car was done right?"

"Aah I was forgetting. I'm just the chauffeur arn't I."

"Know your place daddy."

"Oh I do Logan. Pfft."

Thirteen . . .

"Hello Logan."

"Daddy! What is you doing? You is a crinnimul and you is in jail!"

"What?"

I has seen your FB page and you is in jail so you is a crinnimul!"

"The word is, criminal not crinnimul."

"Whatever daddy. Has you exscaped? You has a crinnimul suit on."

"Logan. I'm not in jail!

"Yes you is. It must be true I reads it on FB."

"Let me explain dog."

"I is going to call the cops!"

"Logan. Knock it off."

"I has my paws on the 999 button!"

"Right. Stop it dog."

"Hand over the treats or I calls the cops!"

"LOGAN!! I'm not in jail. I'm here.

"I can sees that silly." Has you exscaped?"

"Aaargh." It's only FB jail dog! It's not real jail."

"We'll why is you wearing that silly suit?"

"It's a fire proof suit that I have to wear for work."

"You looks like a prisoner.... or maybe a clown."

"Hey. Watch it dog!"

"I still has my paws on the cops number!"

Where is the treats hooman?"

"Okay, Okay I'll get you some treats."

"Good job. Now off you go, into the kitchen and bring back a hand full of treats. There's a good hooman."

" Fine. Here you are enjoy your treats. Would you have called the cops Logan?"

"Try me daddy."

"I think I've just been blackmailed by my dog!"

Fourteen . . .

"Fank yous for leaving me extra foods today while you wents to work daddy."

"You're welco . . . Hey what extra food?"

"That big salami sossy fingy."

"I don't remember leaving you anything extra?"

"It made a nice change from the sammiches."

"Eh. What sammiches? What sossys?"

"The ones you left on the chair in the dining room.

"I didn't leave any.... what have you done dog?"

"I founds some sossy roll fingys on my chair in the dining room."

"What? Don't tell me.....

"They wuz on my chair so they is mine!"

"You've stolen a full salami haven't you!"

"Nope. I tolds you it wuz on my chair so it's mine!"

"I thought it was the 5 second rule in doggy law!"

"Yes it is but while I is here we also has Logans law. Anyfinks on my chair is mine!"

"Those were meant for you new doggy friend Happy. They were supposed to be a present for him off us as a family."

"How was I supposed to know that?"

"I hope you're proud of yourself Logan."

"Well now you come to mention it... I is rather happy, although I couldn't eats a full one. Next time could you take it outs of the packet and slice it up as I struggled a little bit. I did finally manage to get it outs tho. I is a persistent hound don't you fink daddy. " 😠😠😠😠

Fifteen . . .

Ok hooman. What's this all about then?"

"What is your problem now Logan?"

"I is wet!"

"Yep. That's what happens when you go out in the rain."

"You knows I hates water."

"oh I know only too well dog. I've seen you dancing round puddles because you don't want to get your paws wet."

"I doesn't know how deep those puddles is and I may drowns!"

"Now you're just being silly."

"Why is I out in the rains?"

"Because YOU whined to go for a walk, so here we are."

"Yes but it shouldn't be raining when I is out!"

"Well, you wouldn't get wet if you would wear a jacket would you!"

"I hates wearing those things. They used to makes me wear one when I wuz a racer. I used to chew them offs before they coulds put me in the traps!

"I understand that Logan but you have to have one to keep you dry."

"I still hates them."

"We have bought you no less than 4 jackets and you won't wear them. You just sulk like a child but it's for your own good. How many have you chewed off?"

"Oh god hooman. We has had this conversation before. I is a dog and I can'ts count."

"The first one you refused point blank to walk in and tried to chew it off! The 2nd one I had to carry around everywhere because you sulked like a child when you wore it. Your house coat you chewed off. Now you have a wax cotton jacket that spends most of its life hung up behind the damn door!"

"You're just not learning are you hooman."

"Aaaargh. Dog you will be the ruin of me."

"But you do loves me."

"Yes we do Logan."

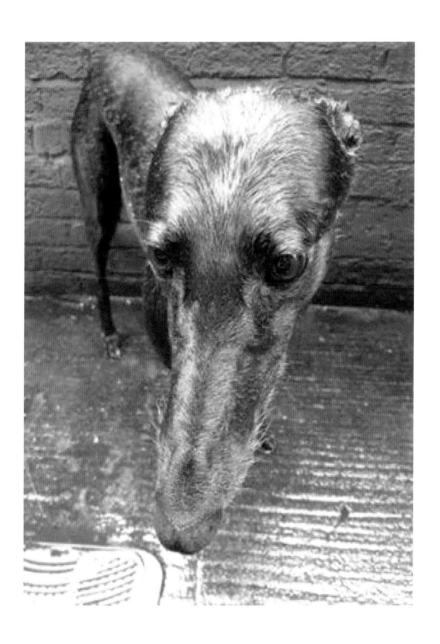

Sixteen . . .

"Daddy."

"Yes Logan?"

"I finks I is poorly and ill and sicks."

"Whatever is the matter with my puppy dog?"

"My tummy keeps making funny noises and I feels like bleurgh."

"I think a trip to the vets is on the cards then eh."

"What!"

"Yep. We'd better take you in and get you checked out. It will involve taking your temperature and possibly an injection plus some medicine."

"Injection!! What for?"

"It will help get you back on your paws again."

"I finks I doesn't needs an injections."

"Ok we'll tell the vet. Don't forget they will still have to take your temperature. Guess how they do that Logan?"

"Dunno daddy?"

"They stick a thermometer up your bum."

"WHOAH! No way!"

"Yes way! Maybe it will stop that smell emanating from your backside eh."

"Daddy."

"Yes Logan.?"

"I finks I is feeling better now."

"I know. Let's put it down to you over eating eh.

"I hasn't."

"Ok. It's the vets for you my lad."

" Well maybe just a little daddy."

"Hmmm. Let's see. You had your tuna mayonnaise sammiches at 4.30 when I got home (one of which ended up buried in our bed!) Then you had your tea (a bowl of dog food.) Followed by a pork sammich. Am I correct?"

"Only one tuna sammich coz I saved the other one for later."

"So, I found out dog! Then mummy fed you again without me knowing. Finally, you had a knuckle bone (again, said bone ended up in our bed!)

"I wuz pacing myself daddy."

"Logan. We both know the reason you are sick is because you've over eaten. AGAIN!" Looks like we need to put you back on a diet."

"Ha. try it fat boy."

"What?"

"Nuffink daddy. It was my tummy growling again." 😄😄

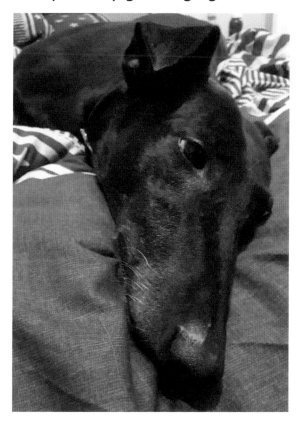

Seventeen . . .

"Helooo laydees in Rintintin land. My name is Logan. I is 8 years old and as you can see I sleeps naked (That's wivsout a collar on.) I has my own place wivs 2 bedrooms right in the centre of town. I is looking for . . ."

"WHOAAH. STOP RIGHT THERE DOG!

"Quiet daddy you is cramping my style."

Nope. It's not happening. Not on this page!"

"It's my page daddy."

"I don't care . . . Anyway. what's Rintintin?"

"It's kind of like Tinder but for houndies."

"I'm confused Logan?"

"It's a dating site for us dogs. You know.. Swipes right and all that stuff."

"Nope. Still no idea what you're on about."

"Oh come on daddy. You is old so you must have tried it."

"Eh?"

"Dating daddy."

"Stop it dog. Besides, I loves your mummy."

"I has needs daddy."

"There's no need to even go there on your Facebook page. This is a houndie friendly, family page. We don't do that here!"

"It's my page daddy!"

"I don't care. Besides, you're nearly 11 years old not 8 years old!"

"Everyone knocks a few years off on these sites daddy. Anyhow, I isn't really that grey so I coulds pass for 8 years old."

"We are not even discussing this on your page Logan!"

"Well, obviously we are aren't we daddy."

"Can we stop this rubbish right now dog. Take your profile off Rintintin or whatever dating site you're on immediately. You're not 11 you're 8 years old. You don't sleep naked just because you have no collar on. Finally, you don't own a 2 bedroomed house in the centre of town!"

"Daddy."

"What now dog?"

"Does I eat where I want, when I want?"

"Yes Logan."

"Does I sleeps where I want when I wants?"

"Yes Logan."

"Does I get my own way all day and every day?"

"Pretty much dog."

"And you don't finks I own the house?"

"With that train of thought I suppose you do. Back to the Rintintin profile. You're going to take it down?"

"Relax daddy. I just made that rubbitch up to show you who's the boss."

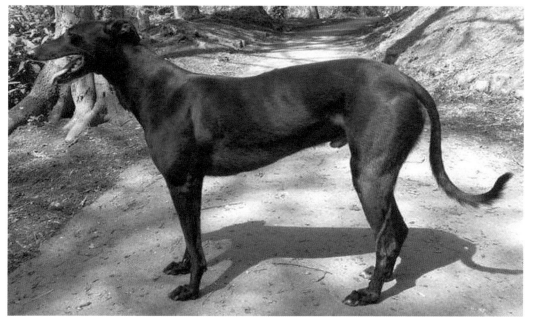

Eighteen . . .

"Daddy."

"Evening Logan."

"Never mind the niceties daddy. What's this in my bowl?"

"It's food Logan."

"Very funny daddy. What kind?"

"It's mince Logan."

"Are you sure daddy?"

"Yep."

"Hmmm. What kind?"

"It's mince fit for a king."

"What kind!!!"

"Dunno Logan."

"Where dids it come from?"

"Mummy got it out of the refrigerator."

"What's a refrigerator?"

"The silver fingy."

"Aaah right."

"Go ahead and tuck in."

Don't fink so daddy."

"Why what's wrong now?"

"Sumfink isn't right."

"It's good mince."

"I has thousands of receptors in my nose and it doesn't smell right!"

"Maybe it's doggy mince?"

"I smells a rat!"

"Oh I'm sure it isn't one of those."

"Very funny daddy. You is trying to con me isn't you!"

"It's mince dog!"

"Receptors daddy!!"

"Oh just eat it you picky hound."

"I will not. Not until you tells me what it is!"

"Nanna sent it so it must be good."

"Stop avoiding the question daddy."

"Ok I'll tell you."

"I'm waiting!!"

"It's quorn mince."

"I knew it. You has tried con me!"

"It's good stuff Logan."

"Nope."

"Look dog you have 2 choices. Take it or leave it!"

"I'm off to see mummy."

"What does that mean?"

"It means you has 2 choices."

Like what?"

"Eat it yourself or chuck it in the bin!"

"Mmmmm Quorn."

"You're going to have to be smarter than that to outwit me daddy and somehow I don't finks it's going to happen is it."

"I'll chuck it in the bin should I Logan?"

"Yes daddy."

"Consider it done dog."

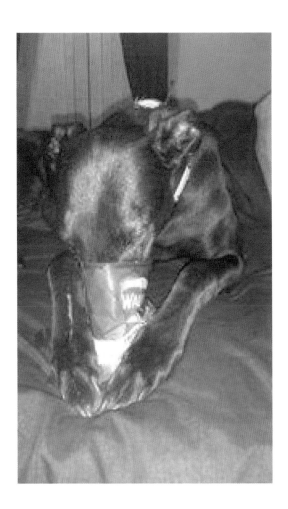

Nineteen . . .

"I is not a happy hound!"

"It's for your own good Logan."

"How does I know that? I doesn't even know what it is."

"Just some drops."

"What kind of drops?"

"Drop drops."

"I smells a rat daddy!"

"Nothing to do with rats Logan."

"You knows exactly what I mean daddy. Don't be trying to fools me. I wants to know what it is."

"It's part of your treatment dog."

"But I isn't ill daddy."

"I know but...."

"No buts daddy. I wants to know right now what it is!"

"It's Errrm. Hmmm."

"NOW DADDY!!"

"It's flea treatment."

"How dares you!"

"We do it every 6 months dog."

"I hasn't got fleas!!!"

"I know you haven't."

"Then why daddy?"

"To make sure you never get them."

"I has never had them, ever!"

"Again, you are right."

"Then it's haminal cruelty. I demand retribution!"

"How does a jumbone, some meaty strips and a doggy sausage sound?"

"And ear rubs!"

"And ear rubs."

"It's a start daddy."

Twenty . . .

"Really dog?"

"What's wrong now daddy?"

"It's 12.30 at night and you've decided You're going to eat a knuckle bone."

"Midnight snack daddy."

"You've brought it upstairs into the bedroom!"

"Yes daddy. MY BEDROOM!"

"No Logan it's our bedroom."

"Yes and this is my part of the bedroom."

"I know but..."

"No buts daddy. I is dining!"

"Look Logan, we both know what's going to happen don't we."

"Yes daddy. I'm going to eats my bone and you will go to sleep."

"How are we supposed to sleep with you gnawing on that thing?"

"No idea daddy."

"Can you not.... "

"No daddy. Whatever you wants the answer is No!"

"I need to go to sleep!"

"I isn't stopping you."

"At some point you're going to try and smash that bone against the wardrobe arn't you."

"There is every possibility daddy."

"Then you're going to leave it in the middle of the floor arn't you?"

"Well, I'm certainly not leaving it on my bed am I daddy?"

"You've left them on our bed before now!"

"That's because I doesn't sleep there."

"There's every chance I'm going to kick the darn thing in the middle of the night and break my toe!"

"Not if you watch where you're walking."

"It will be pitch black dog."

"Yes I know. It's my early warning system."

"What?"

"It's simple daddy, Just like you."

"Explain please."

"When I is asleep you will gets up in the middle of the night, kick the bone, break your toe and scream. That will in turn wake me up and I will move out of the way so you don't stand on me in the dark."

"Brilliant Logan, just brilliant."

Twenty One . . .

"Aaand what time do you call this Logan?"

"I has no idea daddy."

"It's late!"

"Look daddy I has no idea because I is a dog. We doesn't keep track of time!"

"It's nearly 11 o'clock in the morning. You've been in bed since last night."

"Quiet daddy, I is tired."

"How can you be,you've slept longer than I have."

"I hads a busy day yesterday."

"Doing what?"

"I wuz gardeninks at nannas, alright!"

"Aaah yes. Don't we know it!"

"Looks daddy. Nanna said she wanted help digging up the weeds in the garden!"

"Not quite sure you helped there did you dog."

"Nanna gave me 2 big sosigs for helping her so I must have done the right thing."

"She gave you the sausage before you "Helped with the gardening."

""It doesn't matter!"

"Logan. The garden looks like a bomb site!"

"But are there any weeds left?"

"Well, No."

"There you go then!"

Twenty Two . . .

"Afternoon Logan. What would you like for dinner?"

"I finks I shall has fish daddy."

"And how would you like that cooking?"

"I has no idea daddy. Call mummy she will know."

"Hiya Lynn, How does Logan have his fish cooked?"

"First of all, make sure it's fully defrosted."

"Ok, I've done that."

"Get a baking tray and cover it with kitchen foil."

"Got ya."

"Then place some cardboard on the top, place the fish on top so it doesn't retain the water."

"What?"

"Just do as you is told daddy! I likes nice fish."

"Quiet dog."

"Right when you have done that place some more kitchen foil over the top and steam it in the oven for about 20 -30 minutes."

"Errm, this is Logans dinner we're talking about."

"Daddy. Will you just listens! I isn't eating rubbitch!"

"He likes it flaky not soggy."

"Fine!"

"Oh and don't forget to boil him some pasta to go with it."

"Really?"

"Yes I likes fish and pasta."

"Why can't you just have dog food like the rest of them?"

"Because you decided to ask me what I wants and I wants fish! Now hop to it daddy coz I is getting hungry!"

"I'm just a slave in this house ain't I Logan?"

"Now daddy that's the second dumb question you has asked in the last 5 minutes. The first one was "What would you like for dinner?" Will you ever learn?"

"Obviously not dog."

Twenty- Three . . .

"Good morning Logan."

"Go away daddy!"

"What's up now dog?"

"I is under specific instructions not to talk to you."

"Eh?"

"Look daddy. Doggit and Scratcher my solicitors has advised me not to speak to you coz you is a CRINIMAL!"

"The word is criminal not crinimal."

"Whatever daddy. You shoulds be in jail."

"What!"

"I has seen the photo and read it on your FB page. You shoulds be in jail!"

"Oh, if you saw it on FB it must be true then eh Logan."

"It is. So I has no idea what you is doing here. Has you exscaped?"

"No Logan."

Well how come you is here then?"

"Because it's FB jail not real jail you dumbo."

"Of course it's real!! I has lots of friends on FB and they is real."

"I know but..."

"Well there you go then."

"Look dog. It just means I can't post anything."

"I'm calling the cops daddy."

"Why?"

I has told you. You is an exscaped prisoner and you is on the run. It's my duty as a good houndie to do it."

"It's not real jail!"

"Look daddy, my FB friends is real arn't they."

"Yes of course they are."

"You is real ain't you daddy."

"Yes of course I am."

"Then FB jail is real. I'm calling the cops!

"I give up dog."

"Good. I will gets a reward for capturing a hardant crinimal."

"I'm not a crinimal. Logan I'm your father!"

"Now you sound likes Darth Vader." "Logan. I am your father."

"How did we get from FB jail to Star Wars?"

"Because you exscaped! Hello, is that the local police station?

"Yes it is."

"Can you come quickly my daddy has gone crazy. He's exscaped prison and now he finks he's Darth Vader!"

"Aaargh! You drive me nuts Logan."

"Oh it's waaay to late for that daddy." 🙂

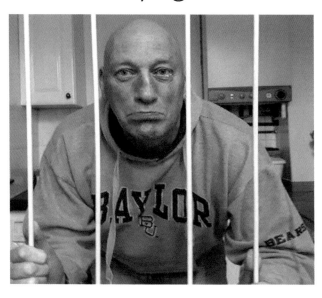

Twenty Four . . .

"Are you comfortable there Logan?"

"Quiet daddy I has had a very busy and very stressful day so now I needs some "me time."

"Doing what?"

"I helped you wivs the fundraising auction first thing this morning. "

"How?"

"Well I didn't keeps whining to go out for a pee and poop."

"That's true."

"Then we wents to "Animals in distress" charity shop."

"Again, you are correct dog."

"Followed by a walk round Blackleach country park and lunch at nanna's."

"Remind me what happened there Logan."

"I wuz attacked!"

"By "attacked" you actually mean you decided to stick your nose where you shouldn't have done. Then you managed to get your paw caught in the coat pocket of nannas coat which was hanging on the back of the chair, which in turn caused you to howl the place down! How you managed that I will never know."

"As I said . . . I wuz attacked!

"Next stop on the list?"

"A sneaky trip to the vets which wuz sprung on me by an unscrupulous hooman! Note to self . . . call Doggit and Scratcher!"

"No Logan. You had to go because your eye is sore and weeping."

"I was weeping because I was cruelly tricked into going to the vets!"

"Stop playing the sympathy card dog. You had to go!"

"If you say so daddy."

"First job at the vets? The weigh in!"

"Again. Done under duress!"

"Again. Done because it needs doing. Guess what we learned?"

"That I doesn't like going to the vets?"

"We already knew that. What we actually learned was . . . You lost 2 and a half kilos when you had gastric trouble."

"That's a good thing daddy."

"Let me finish dog! You have put a kilo back on you little porker."

"I looked unnatural daddy."

"You looked like a greyhound!"

"Daddy. Do you know why I is on the couch?"

"Because you're tired as you've had a busy day."

"No. It's so I can put the cushions over my head so I doesn't has to listen to your rubbitch!"

"I'll shut up then eh?"

"Finally!"

Twenty Five . . .

"You're up early Logan?"

"I has fings to do daddy."

"But we're on lockdown."

"Well you may be but I isn't so open the door and let me out!"

"Ok dog whatever you want. By the way, where are you off to?"

"I is off to the park daddy."

"What on earth for?"

"Seeing as how the local council isn't working, I has a job to do."

"Like what?"

"I is the self-appointed gardener."

"Eh?"

"See you later daddy I has chores to do."

"Whatever dog."

15 minutes later . . .

"Whoaah. Wait a minute!"

"Hello daddy. What kept you?"

"Ok dog what have you done now?"

"Gardeninks daddy."

"Gardeninks?"

"Yes daddy. Take a look."

"Dear god dog. There are whacking great holes everywhere!"

"Yes daddy. I has made the park dog friendly."

"By digging holes?"

"Yep. Now all my doggy friends will has somewhere cool to lie during the hot weather."

"I'll get a shovel and fill them all in before anyone sees it."

"Just call me "Capability Hound" famous doggy gardener."

Twenty Six . . .

"Nanna."

"Yes Logan."

"Does you loves me?"

"Yes of course I do puppy dog."

"Nanna."

"Yes Logan."

"Is I your favourite grandoggy?"

"You're my only grandoggy Logan."

"What are you up to dog?"

"Quiet Daddy I is working!"

"Nanna."

What can I do for you puppy?"

"Can I has a treat please nanna?"

"Yes of course you can."

"Fank yous nanna."

"Now I want a doggy kiss."

"Awww does I have to?"

"If you want another treat I want a doggy kiss."

"You know I doesn't do doggy kisses nanna."

"Ha. It looks like you're in debt to nanna dog."

"Shouldn't you be at work Daddy?"

"I've been to work and now I'm here to collect you. C'mon it's time to go home."

"Wait a minute Logan!"

"Awww nanna I has to go home."

"Not before I get my doggy kiss."

"Pay up dog. Nanna wants a kiss."

"But . . . but . . . Errrm."

"Now Logan!"

"But whiskers will tickle nanna."

"I don't mind Logan."

"Not my whiskers nanna. Yours!"

"I think we'd better go before you get your paws rapped dog!"

"I wuz joking Daddy."

"It's fine puppy. I know it was a joke. Here's a treat for the journey home."

"Fank yous nanna."

"Deary me dog. You can do no wrong in nannas eyes can you?"

"It's the old Logan charm Daddy. It works every time." 😁

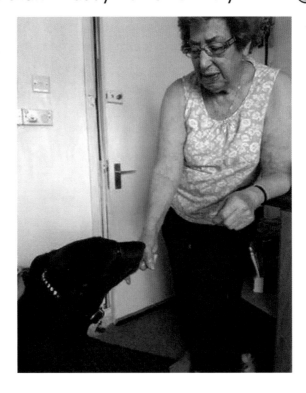

Twenty Seven . . .

"So Logan. Will his lordship be rising today?"

"Does it look like it Daddy?"

"It's nearly lunchtime dog!"

"I has been up first thing this morning!"

"What time was that then?"

"Dunno. It wuz dark and cold tho. Besides, I is a houndie and I has no concept of time."

"Oh I wouldn't say that dog. You certainly know when it's time to eat!"

"Silly Daddy. It's always time to eat."

"In your case that's true. Anyway, are you getting up?"

"Let me finks about it for a while."

"It's lunchtime! Now get up!"

"Are we going anywhere?"

"Yes! We're going to the market for something to eat."

"Will we be calling at Ken's Deli?"

"Possibly."

"Will I gets roast beefs or chicken or hams?"

"Probably. You know he always treats you."

"I shalls be up presently then."

"No rush. Take your time. Whenever it suits you."

"Wake me when have your coat on Daddy."

"Just get up you lazy hound!"

"I has been up and now I is back in bed."

"Move it dog!"

"What's the weather like?"

"It's beautiful bright sunshine so move."

"I'm coming Daddy. Now about that beefs at Ken's....."

"You're just a mercenary aren't you Logan."

"I prefer to call it smart Daddy."

"No arguments from me on that score dog."

"Aaah Ken's Deli. Can I has some hams please Ken?" 😃

Twenty Eight . . .

"I shalls just lie here for a while Daddy."

"Oh really dog?"

"Yes Daddy."

"Why?"

"You spends lots of time on the laptop so I thought I would keep you company for a while."

"It wouldn't have anything to do with the fact that I'm cooking a load of sausages would it now Logan?"

"Of course not Daddy."

"It wouldn't have anything to do with the fact that every time I go into the kitchen I have to step over you?"

"It never crossed my mind."

"So, if I went into the kitchen you wouldn't come haring down to the bottom end to see if I went to your treat box?"

"I isn't hungry Daddy. I has had my eveninks meal and I is relaxing. Well that's if you will let me!"

"Fine. By the way, what have you had?"

"I has had doggy food wivs biccies and ox tongue followed by chicken bites."

"Really?"

"Yes Daddy."

"Well that makes my beans on toast look a bit tame doesn't it."

"That's because we has a pecking order in this house."

"I take it I'm nearer the bottom than the top then?"

"No Daddy you isn't."

"Phew. That's good to know. What would the bottom of the pecking order eat then?"

"Beans on toast Daddy!"

Twenty Nine . . .

"Are you quite comfortable there dog?"

"Yes Daddy."

"Good. You get plenty of rest for the next day or so."

"I has every intention of doing Daddy."

"We have a busy day on Thursday."

"We has?"

"Yep."

"What is we doing?"

"First of all we're going to nannas...."

"That's not busy!"

"Let me finish dog."

"This isn't going to be one of those long drawn out stories is it Daddy? I has napping to do."

"I'll be as quick as I can."

"Get on with it man."

"As I said, we're going to...."

"Yes, yes. I know."

"Then I'm going to the dentist."

"Aaaand that has what to do with me?"

"Because then . . . You're going to the physiotherapist."

"I doesn't need a psycho therapist!"

"Physiotherapist! Will you listen properly!"

"Whatever it is I doesn't need one."

"Yes you do! She is going to help heal your shoulder and stop you limping."

"I is just fine Daddy."

"No you're not."

"Yes I is."

"Well why do you keep limping then?"

"Sympathy Daddy. I gets lots of it when I limp."

"Not anymore you won't!"

"Oh but I wills."

"Not from me you won't."

"I doesn't need it off you Daddy. You is already under the paw."

"No argument from me on that one dog."

"Can I get back to my nap now?"

"Yes if you want to but you're still going for physio on Thursday."

"We'll see."

"Oh but you are!"

"Zzzzzz."

"I take it your asleep then?"

"Zzzzzzz."

"Am I boring you Logan?"

"Every day Daddy. Every day. 🙄

Thirty . . .

"What's wrong with the chicken foot I gave you Logan?"

""I doesn't want it Daddy."

"And why not?"

"It's not to my liking."

"You've eaten them before dog!"

Not anymore Daddy."

"We bought them especially for you as a treat. They're off Debbie on the market. You love her treats because they are all natural."

"Well I has changed and I doesn't want them today!!"

"That doesn't explain why you suddenly won't eat them!"

"I has modified my tastes in life Daddy."

"Oh really. Do tell dog."

"I has got used to the finer things in life."

"You've been to nannas haven't you Logan."

"Don't play dumb wivs me Daddy (although I doubt you is playing.) You knows darn well I has been to nannas!"

"Ok. What has she been feeding you this time? Hot dog sausages?"

"Pfft. Minced up rubbitch! They is not for this hound anymore."

"You love hot dog sosigis Logan."

"Yes but I has gone up in the world."

"How far?"

"I now eats salmon Daddy."

"Really?"

"Yes Daddy."

"Pink or Red?"

"Cucumber!"

"Eh?"

"Cucumber red salmon."

"Wow!"

"Yep. None of that cheap pink salmon for this dog."

"Blimey Logan, you have gone up in the world!"

"You know it Daddy."

"Don't get used to it dog. We ain't buying you red salmon every day!"

"No problem Daddy."

"You took that rather well Logan."

"That's because I can always move to nannas on a permanent basis if you don't up your game Daddy!"

"I should have seen that coming shouldn't I."

"Yes Daddy. You should have also bought me red salmon!!!"

"I can't win can I dog."

"I've been here 6 years and yet, still you try. Some people lives and learns. Not you though eh Daddy." 🤣🤣

Thirty One . . .

"Hello Logan."

"Don't you "Hello Logan" me Daddy!"

"Ok. Good evening Logan."

"Nope. Not good enough!"

"What's wrong puppy dog?"

"That isn't washing wivs me Daddy!"

"What's wrong now?"

"I shalls be calling my solicitors "Doggit and Scratcher" first fing in the morning!"

"Whoah. Slow down there dog."

"I knows that you and mummy is up to sumfink!"

"Like what?"

"I isn't quite sure but sumfink isn't right."

"Like what?"

"Look at me!"

"I am doing. Very handsome you are too Logan."

"I isn't talking about that!"

"Gimme a clue then dog."

"First of all. Since I has been in hospital I has been getting lots of extra treats."

"And you're worth every one of them puppy dog."

"Hmmm. I smells a rat!"

"Why?"

"Because I is smart Daddy!"

"Oh we already know that."

"I has been getting lots of meaty balls and hot dog sosigis."

"Well, that's because you haven't been to nannas since you've been ill so we decided to give you nannas hot dog sosigis so you don't miss her."

"And the meaty balls?"

"Extras for being a very special hound."

"Hmmm. Somehow I doesn't fink so Daddy!"

"You don't believe me do you."

"Not a word Daddy."

"But You love meatballs."

"I has never hads them on a regular basis before. Now you finks it's ok to give them to me. You is feeding me tablets isn't you Daddy!"

"Weeellll."

"Why do you finks I has started chewing the meaty balls? Why do you finks you now has to give me about 3 one after the other?"

Because you're worth it Logan."

"Nope. It's because you finks I wills spit the tablets out don't you?"

"What tablets?"

"The ones you have been giving me for the last couple of weeks!"

"So you knew?"

"Of course I dids!"

"So we've been giving you extra treats for nothing?"

"No Daddy. You has been giving me extra treats because you has been outsmarted." 😁😁

Thirty Two . . .

"Ok numnuts tell everyone what you've done!"

"I hasn't done nuffink Daddy."

"Anything."

"What?"

"You haven't done anything."

"Well why did you ask me in the first place then Daddy?"

"No Logan. The sentence is I haven't done anything. No double negatives."

"I know I haven't."

"There you go."

"Daddy."

"Yes Logan."

"Why are we having this conversation?"

"I want you to tell people what you've done."

"Nuffink. I is confined to the house."

"You've been out though haven't you."

"I needed a pee and a poop."

"Aaaand what did you do?"

"I hads a pee and a poop."

"Go on."

"I saw a puddy tat."

"What else?"

"I chased it!"

"You're supposed to be resting! You have a sore wrist you daft dog!"

"I'm a dog. It's what we do Daddy."

"I know but . . ."

"No buts Daddy!"

"I take it you didn't catch it?"

"We doesn't want to catch them silly."

"Well why chase them then?"

"Because it's fun."

"But that's just pointless."

"A bit like this conversation then eh Daddy."

"Look dog, you're supposed to be taking it easy. The physiotherapist said no long walks or strenuous exercise."

"I is bored Daddy."

"It doesn't matter. Just do as you're told for once eh. We just want you fit and well."

"It isn't my fault mummy has washed my teddies on the same day you decided I can't go out is it?"

"Well no but it doesn't mean you have to run around like an eejut does it dog."

"I've told you. Dogs chase puddy tats, puddy tats chase meeces and so on.

"We're just going round in circles here aren't we Logan."

"Yes Daddy."

"I should just give up shouldn't I."

"Yes Daddy."

"Well that's 10 minutes of my life I won't get back!"

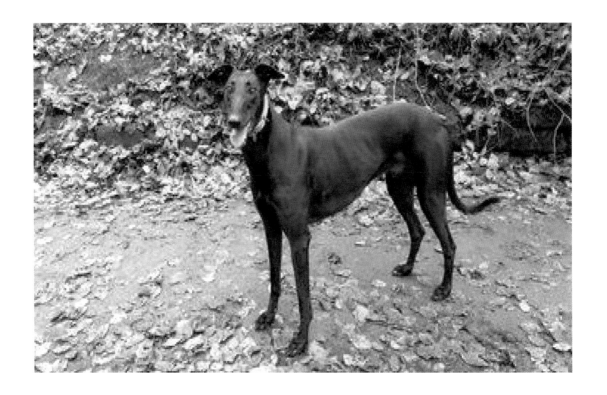

Thirty Three . . .

"What on earth are you doing Logan?"

"I is on guard duty at nanna's."

"I'd hardly call lounging on a scrunched-up duvet guard duty."

"Well, I IS!!"

"Guarding nanna from what?"

"Not Guarding nanna silly. I is guarding the duvet!!"

"Now I know I'm going to regret this but, go on, tell me about it."

"Well, when I gots here this morning nanna said there was a 13 dog duvet in the bedroom."

"A what?"

"Lets me finish Daddy!"

"Ok dog. Carry on."

"As I wuz saying . . . Nanna said there was a 13 dog duvet in the bedroom so I charged upstairs to see who these doggies were. When I gots here the bedroom wuz empty! No doggies. Nuffink."

"Now I'm confused."

"Not as confused as I am Daddy. Why would nanna say there wuz a 13 dog duvet in here when there isn't?"

"No idea Logan."

"Well ifs they turn up I shalls be waiting for them! They isn't sharing my duvet!"

"Wait a minute!"

"Look Daddy. I isn't moving from here. It doesn't matter what you say!"

"Now I get it. It's a 13 TOG duvet not 13 dog duvet you cloth eared hound."

"Whether they is dogs, togs or mogs they isn't having my duvet!!"

"Look Logan. The Tog is actually rating for it. It isn't an animal!"

"I doesn't care! I isn't moving!"

"Fine! Stay there then!"

"I wuz going to anyways Daddy."

Thirty Four . . .

Today I has been fundraising for something called Candy Cane. I has no idea what it is but people fed me treats, petted me, stroked me and gave me cuddles. I has been on my paws all day and I is sooo tired. Apparently my daddy can sell sand to the Arabs (whatever that means) Anyway, we made lot's of money for a doggy charity which helps hounds escape the dog meat trade in China! 😞😞😞 Off to put my paws up and have a nice long nap.

Thirty Five . . .

So, there I was lounging around at nanna's on my day of rest. Nanna decides she's going out to play bingo (whatever that is) for a couple of hours. I thinks to myself " time to investigate things." After snuffling arounds for a while I decided to go upstairs for even more looksees. Weeelll guess what I found Tucked down behind a computer desk? Only a bag full of treats! Yaaay. I finks nanna must have been hiding them in case any hobbirel person breaks in and steals them. Maybe she's forgotten about them? Either way I has liberated them. They now has teef marks in them so everyone will knows they are mine. 😊😊

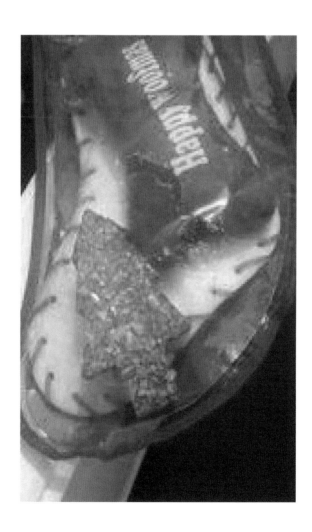

Thirty Six . . .

"Where is you going hoomans?"

"Oh just out for an hour or so."

"That's why you has given me this bone isn't it!"

"Errm... hmmm."

Do you think you can bribes me wiv this large slow roasted bone?"

"Yes!"

"But I is giving you the sad eyes and everyfink."

"So you don't want the bone then? Should we stay in and put the bone back in the oven and we'll stay in?"

"Don't be silly. I knows you will be back in a while then we wills go to the chippy and I will gets a large sossy"

"Maybe we won't go to the chippy tonight Logan."

"Silly hoomans. If I knows this bone is a bribe, I'm damn sure I knows we are going to the chippy later."

"Point taken."

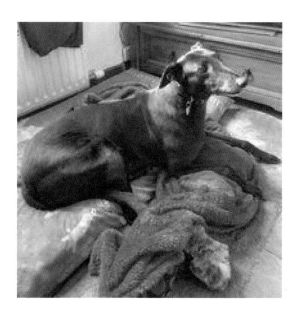

Thirty Seven . . .

"Daddy! You said we wuz going for our normal Sunday morning walk!!"

"And we have done. You've been out with all your friends and had a walk in the woods."

"You never said anyfinks about going shopping."

"It was a spur of the moment thing buddy."

"Why is my car full of all this rubbitch?"

"It isn't rubbitch."

"Well what is it then?"

"It's food and other supplies that we need."

"Why does I has to be shopping wivs you?"

"Because I'm not suffering alone dog."

"You isn't suffering tho is you."

"Oh I am Logan."

"Well why doesn't you come and lie in the back with all this rubbitch?"

"Because I have to drive the car. Anyway some of the food is yours!"

"It is?"

"Yes. Doggy food, doggy biccies, doggy treats and we've even got you some sardines."

"Can I has sardines when we gets home?"

"Yes if you want to Logan."

"Good. I likes sardines."

"Are we forgiven then?"

"Hmmm I will finks about it daddy. (I will also finks about wiping my chops all over the furniture when you isn't looking)

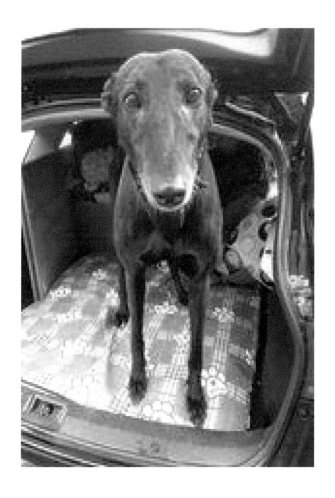

Thirty Eight . . .

"Look at this Logan."

What has you got there daddy?"

"It's your adoption information and photos."

"Wow. They must have caught me on a bad day!"

"Oh I dunno dog."

"I looks like a goofball."

"Nah."

"Is you blind? Looks at it! My ears are all floppy and my tongue is hanging out!"

"If I were you I'd be more bothered about the description."

"It says stunning black boy. I is one of those."

"Yeah but it also says "great with people."

"I was."

"So what happened then?"

"I gots old and grumpy just like you daddy!"

"I have no answer to that."

"As I said... Old and grumpy. Game set and match to me eh daddy."

"Pretty much dog, pretty much."

Thirty Nine . . .

"I see you're enjoying your bone Logan."

"Yes I is."

"Good. It's nice to see you happy."

"I will be much happier when I gets that chicken out of the fridge."

"What chicken?"

"That cooked chicken that mummy bought the other day when we was fundraising."

"I don't remember that?"

"I does! It's in the fridge coz I saw her puts it there."

"You know too much dog."

"I also know that I will be getting some in my bowl later."

"And how would you know that Logan?"

"Because if it doesn't appear I shall go on fundraising strike."

"No you won't. Oh and don't bother calling Doggit and Scratcher your lawyers because you haven't been mistreated in any way shape or form."

"Hello, is that the RGU?"

"Stop right there dog!"

"Quiet daddy I is on the phone!"

"Who to now?"

"The Retired Greyhound Union"

"Who?"

"He is my union rep. I needs to know if I is within my rights to withdraw my Labour if I doesn't get chicken which was bought during fundraising time of which I was an integral part."

"WHAAAT!"

"I knows my rights."

"You are part of a union?"

"Yep."

"What part of the cooked chicken do you want?"

"I knew you'd see it my way daddy."

Bloody hell. My dog is Cavanaugh QC and Arthur Scargill rolled into one! 😴

Forty . . .

"Daddy we needs to talk!!"

"Ok. As long as it's not the birds and the bees thing."

"What?"

"Never mind. Go ahead dog, what's wrong?"

"Is I family?"

"Of course you are puppy dog."

"Good. I is having my say then!"

"Fire away dog."

"The other day you came home very very late and I isn't happy!"

"I'd only been to the pub with Hamish McHamish."

"I doesn't care. You shouldn't be so lates on a school night!"

"I wasn't working so it didn't matter."

"Yes it does. I didn't gets my late night walk."

"It was raining hard so you won't go out anyway."

"Not the point!"

"Yes it is."

"And anovver fing."

"What now?"

"You wuz drunks and you smelled funny."

"No I wasn't and no I didn't."

"Yes you dids!"

"That's rich coming from you. The hound that can clear a house with one fart!"

"YOU SMELLED FUNNY!!"

"Like what?"

"You has been wivs another doggy!"

"Sometimes your friend Happy comes into the pub."

"Nope. I smells his bum most weeks and it wasn't him!"

"Oh please Logan. We don't need to know that."

"Who was it?"

"I did stroke Niamh Whites doggy. She brought him into the pub while she was working."

"Listen. Does I smells other hoomans when you're not there?"

"I wouldn't know would I dog."

"I doesn't! It's not the doggy way!!"

"So what's the upshot of all this then Logan?"

"I is disowning you."

"What?"

"Hello is that Doggit and Scratcher, divorce lawyer to the high class hounds?"

"Shall I pack your case Logan?"

"No. I hads a word with mummy and it's cheaper to gets rid of you! "Shall I pack your case daddy?"

Forty One . . .

"Oh my god Logan are you ok!!"

"I finks I will live."

"I just heard the "greyhound scream of death" is everything alright?"

"It's nothing really."

"No, please tell me. Are you sure you haven't injured yourself?"

"It wuz pretty serious but I finks will live."

"What happened puppy dog?"

"Well, I climbed all the way upstairs, and, and . . ."

"Do we need to call a vet?"

"Vets!!!"

"Yes Logan, if you've had a major accident that calls for the 'greyhound scream of death' it must be serious."

"I shalls struggle on daddy."

"What happened after you reached the top of the stairs?"

"I gots into the bedroom and my cooling fan wasn't on!!"

"Is that it??"

"What do you mean. "Is that it?" I could have died!"

"Of what?"

"Houndie overheating."

"You've climbed the stairs and that's it Logan."

"Yes, but the ambient temperature is different at altitude and seeing as how us greyhounds have a heartbeat twice fast as any other hound it affects me greater than any hooman or haminal!"

"So, why the greyhound howl of death then?"

"Turn my fan on please daddy."

"It's on Logan. Now, why the howl of death then?"

"I caught my dew claws on my duvet."

"You're trying my patience dog!"

"Every day daddy." 😊😊

Forty Two . . .

A political party broadcast on behalf of the Houndie party.

Could I be the next prime minister? I finks I could be.

Are you tired of our government and all the grey areas about covid? Are you fed up with being hounded into doing things you shouldn't have to? Are you always in the doghouse with your friends because of your political views? When you whine does your local council never listen? Is your local MPs bark worse than his bite or is he just toothless? Don't get collared by people with street corner political views. Vote for a new lead(er.) Vote for someone who gets his teeth into his work. Vote for someone who will treats you right. Vote for someone who is very dogmatic. Vote Boris Auty Houghton!

Forty Three . . .

"Good Morning Logan."

"Go away Daddy."

"No Logan. Guess what it is..."

"It's today Daddy. now let me go back to sleep."

""Eh?"

"It's today. Yesterday was a today, Tomorrow will be a today when it gets here and today is today."

"Blimey! I never thought of it like that."

"Can I go back to sleep now Daddy?"

"No Logan. It's Sunday. It's walking day with all your friends."

"Not yet it isn't."

"Why not?"

"Because I is still sleeping! that makes it still yesterday."

"Aaah but you're awake. So that makes it today. Ha. Got you!"

"It isn't today until I gets out of bed!"

"You're just trying to confuse me aren't you dog."

"That wouldn't be hard now would it Daddy."

"Well, no but . . ."

"Is Conrad here wivs my treats?"

"No not yet. He will be here in about an hour."

"Well that's when it's today."

"You're hard work Logan. That's what you are."

"No Daddy. I'm sleeping. You're just making it hard work. Now run along and I shalls have another hour until Conrad gets here wivs the treats."

"So you're staying there then?"

"I thought I'd made that quite clear over the last 5 minutes!"

"I don't know why I even bother dog."

"Neither do I Daddy. Neither do I." 😔😔

Forty Four . . .

"What a Swizz! We is in Robin Hoods bay and I has searched high and low but there's no sign of him. The only fings I could see is the sea and lots of little houses. That's all very well if you is a mini hooman or a fish. Speaking of fish, we saws a building wivs a dolphin on it, guess what? NO DOLPHINS!!!"

"Logan. The Dolphin was the name of a pub!"

"I might have known daddy! It's still a Swizz! I has been cheated. 😡😡

"No you haven't. Anyway, we're off to pastures new tomorrow."

"Pastures new. Does that means we will see cows?"

"Hmmm. Possibly."

"I wants to see cows! It's my hollibobs too you know."

"Why would you need to see cows anyway, we have them at home."

"Because I didn't see Robin Hood or dolphins!"

"You know dog, it's only the first day of the holiday and I'm tired."

"Me too daddy. Nap time now."

Forty Five . . .

"Our second walkies today and we went through Borsdane Wood. I loves it in here coz there are loads of squirrels to chase."

"Not that you ever catch any though is it dog?" 😒

"I doesn't want to catch them daddy!"

"Just as well eh Logan. I mean, if we had to rely on you catching our food we'd starve in a week."

"Feeding me is your job daddy. My job is to protect the house and keeps you hoomans in line."

"Well you're pretty good at the second one son."

"If you wuz a bit smarter daddy I wouldn't has to spend so much time doing the second one so I would have more time to guard the house!"

"If you spent less time asleep we'd all be happier dog."

"I needs to conserve energy just in case we has a break in."

"Really?"

"Yes daddy. Besides, the longer I'm awake the more time I will have to annoy you."

"Good point dog."

"Right. It's nap time. Be a good man and lets me know when dinner is served eh."

"What happened to you being a guard dog then?"

"I tolds you. I'm conserving energy. Besides, you is at home so if anyone comes through the door you can bites them."

"You're all heart Logan."

"It's called "job sharing" daddy. Times are hard during lockdown. You should be glad to have job."

"I really should shouldn't I."

"Yes! Now can I has a bit of quiet while I has my nap?"

"Certainly your lordship." 😔😔

Forty Six . . .

A short story in words and pictures . . .

"Is we going out for a walk daddy?"

"Yes if you want to Logan."

"Wait a minute daddy. Just lets me check the weather."

"You have a waterproof jacket dog!"

"I isn't wearing that!"

"So, are we going out or what?"

"A quick check out of the window. Aaand it's raining so that will be a big fat NO!"

Forty Seven . . .

DID YOU KNOW???

Greyhounds almost died out during the Middle Ages, but clergymen preserved the breed. Subsequently, only nobles owned the breed, which England's King Canute codified in 1014, ruling that only nobles were allowed to have greyhounds. The dogs were considered more valuable than serfs, and anyone responsible for killing a greyhound faced execution.

Forty Eight . . .

"It's very humid today Logan."

"You is humid every day daddy."

"No I'm not."

"Yes you is!

"How can I be humid when it's cold Logan?"

"Cold?"

"Yes Logan. When the temperature drops and you're no longer a hot dog."

"You has hot dogs???"

"No Logan. You are a hot dog. You know, when it's warm and you start panting. That's when we put the fan on you to stop you over heating. That's humid."

"When can I has hot dog sossies?"

"You can't."

"So, you is humid and I is a hot dog but I can't have any sossies."

"I'm confused now dog."

"Well you started it daddy."

"I just said that it was humid"

"I know you is a humid. Mummy is a humid too."

"You mean human!"

"Yes. The plural of human is humids"

"No it isn't dog."

"Well I says it is!"

"I stand corrected and I'm glad we got that cleared up."

"Now about these hot dog sossies!"

"There are no hot dog sossies. The hot dog is you!"

"No I isn't."

"Yes you are. I've had to put the fan on for you."

"So there are no sossies then?"

"No!"

"Are there any other treats?"

"Logan."

"Yes daddy?"

"This conversation has given me a headache. If I give you a treat can we just sit and watch TV?"

"Treats is like humids daddy."

"What?"

"They come in more than one."

"You can have the whole box if we can just end this conversation!"

"Done deal daddy." 😂😂

Forty Nine . . .

"Daddy."

"Yes Logan."

"I has pondered."

"Ok where is it and I'll get a bag?"

"Silly hooman. I said pondered not pooped!"

"Oh right."

"As I said. I has been pondering."

"Aaand what have you been pondering about?"

"Well. You know I has been retired from racing for a long time now."

"Yes. It's nearly 5 years Logan."

"I finks it's time I was off to see the world."

'What!" "Yep. I has packed a suitcase and I is going."

"But you have lots of holidays with us."

"I knows but I finks it's time I streched my paws before I gets too old to travel."

"You do plenty travelling with us. Plus You get to sit in the car (even when we're not going anywhere.) and watch the world go by."

"Yes I do buts I needs to explore on my own."

"What about all your doggy friends here?"

"Shall sends them all a pawscard."

"Awe don't go Logan. We'll all miss you too much."

"I has made up my mind."

"Look. No one wants you to go. Mummy and I love you so much."

"Hmmm. If I stays I will be giving up my puppyhood dream of travelling the world."

"Ok whatever you want it's yours. Just stay here."

"Anyfinks?"

"Anything you want."

"Lets me see. Errrm. Hmmmm."

"Well?"

"Treats!"

"Ok we can do that."

"No more of this diet fingy."

"But it's for your own good."

"NO MORE DIETS!"

"Ok, we'll just monitor what you eat."

"I cans live wivs that."

"So you're staying here then?"

"Yes daddy."

"Awwwe that's great news. Shall I put your suitcase away?"

"My suitcase?"

"Yes the one by your side."

"Oh this isn't mine."

"Well who's is it then?"

"It's mummies case. Conrad is using it to go on his hollibobs." 😵😵😵

"So you just used it to get your treats back and get off your diet!!!"

"I didn'ts say "this" was my case did I daddy?"

"Oooo. That's just downright devious dog!"

"Nope. It's smart daddy. Besides. It's raining out and you know how much I hates water."

"You conniving, hound you!!!"

"If you're going into the kitchen grab me some treats." 😋😋😋

Fifty . . .

"Here daddy I has brought you sumfink for daddy's day."

"You mean fathers day?"

"Daddy, father. Whatever."

"It's a bit late. It was on Sunday."

"You didn'ts gives me any pawcket money until Monday!"

"Well that's true. I see they have been opened."

"Yes daddy. Quality assurance. I has to test them."

"Riiight."

"They is fine and not poisonous."

"Well thank you for my present Logan."

"Aah it's no problem daddy."

"You're a dog in a million Logan."

"I knows and you is a daddy in a million. Now can we stop talking and eats them coz I is starvinks. 😁😁"

"Why do I think I've just been hoodwinked by a dog? Doh"

Fifty One . . .

"Ok Logan what are you doing?"

"I is on paw patrol daddy."

"Which means what?"

"I goes round to all the neighbours houses to checks them all."

"Check them for what?"

"Oh you know, to make sure everyfink is all right and fings."

"Hmmm. I smell a rat!"

"You do?"

"Yes Logan."

"Well it's a good jobs I is on patrol then eh daddy. Points me in the right direction and I shall sees him off!"

"Not that kind of rat."

"There's another kind?"

"Nevermind dog."

"Well, be on your way daddy. I is a busy hound. I has to visit all the neighbours to check everyfink out."

"There's something fishy going on here!"

"Nope. No fish only... Errrm cough cough."

"Aha! What did you nearly say then?"

"Nuffink daddy. I just had a furball."

"What are you really doing?"

"Well if you must know I'm visiting Beryl and Clive. Then I needs to check on Debbie and John before finally checking in on Wayne and Kath at the shop."

"You seem to have a lot of friends that you need to check in with Logan."

"Oh yes daddy. I is very busy now go away."

"You're after treats ain't you dog!"

"Me! Would I ever? Honestly daddy, does you not trust me?"

"Well lets put it this way. You have been on a diet for about 3 months now and not lost a pound, so something is amiss."

"I is just big boned daddy."

"The neighbours are giving you treats aren't they!"

"No daddy. It's payment for doing my paw patrol and protecting their houses and businesses."

"I knew it. You've been playing the sympathy card haven't you."

"Is it my fault I is a handsome houndie wivs puppy dog eyes?"

"Get your ass in here NOW!

"But I hasn't finished my rounds yet."

"I'll give you the rounds of the kitchen if you don't get in this house now my lad."

"I don't suppose that while we're in the kitchen you could open my treats box and maybe . . .

"IN! NOW!"

Fifty Two . . .

Lynn goes into the kitchen and 2 minutes later Logan comes charging into the living room like his arse is on fire. His prize? A potato!!! I mean. Seriously dog. It's not like you even like the darn things.

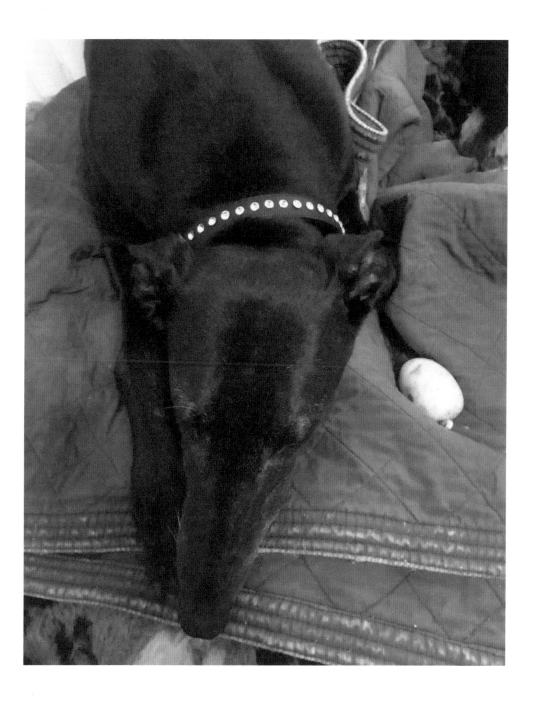

Fifty Three . . .

"Daddy"

"Yes Logan?"

"I finks it's time to leave."

"Leave? Leave what?"

"I finks it's time to leave you and mummy and all my friends."

"But you can't."

"Yes I cans."

"But where will you go?"

"Remember how you hads a star named after me?"

"Yes, it's called Logans Light."

"Well that's where I is going."

"But why?"

"Because I has to go."

"No you don't."

"Don't argue Daddy you wills only lose."

"OK puppy dog. What will you do when you get there?"

"I is a star Daddy. I wills shine bright for thousands of years."

"But you're a star right here."

"I know that Daddy."

"What about all your friends here?"

"I shalls see you all when you comes to join me. Besides, all you has to do is look up at the night sky and there I am watching over everyone."

"But this is your home Logan."

"Oh I isn't leaving altogether."

"You're not?"

"No Daddy. I wills always be here. I is in your heart. I wills be in the house or wherever you all go. You wills see me out of the corner of your eye or when you is asleep I shalls visit you. We never fully leave you. We can't because we has a bond through eternity."

"Now I understand."

"Finally Daddy."

"Yes Logan."

"I has finally trained you and mummy and nanna, so now my job is done."

"Maybe we can find you another job?"

"Don't fink so Daddy. I has been a racing greyhound, A kennel hound, A couch potato, A fundraiser, A gardeninks expert, A zoomie hound and a teacher of hoomans. I finks I has done enough for one lifetime."

"Maybe you could stay just a little longer?"

"No Daddy. As I said before, my job here is done.

Tell mummy and nanna not to cry."

"We're all here for you puppy dog."

"Sends my love to all my friends. Tells them if they miss me, just look for Logans light shining down on them."

"Good night and god bless Logan."

"Night night Daddy."

LOGAN AUTY HOUGHTON 2/10/2009 - 17/05/2021

Printed in Great Britain
by Amazon